P9-DHT-184

Ex-Library: Friends of
Lake County Public Library

Bonnie
Christensen

Dial Books for Young Readers ❖ New York

LAKE COUNTY PUBLIC LIBRARY

3 3113 01648 4331

4 M + ILY,

M + 👁 SWEET 🏠 !

Published by
Dial Books for Young Readers
A Division of Penguin Books USA Inc.
375 Hudson Street
New York, New York 10014

Copyright © 1997 by Bonnie Christensen
All poems by Bonnie Christensen except "Be My Valentine"
(anonymous), the illustrations for which first appeared in
Ladybug magazine in February 1995.
All rights reserved • Designed by Nancy R. Leo
Printed in Hong Kong • First Edition
1 3 5 7 9 10 8 6 4 2

Library of Congress Cataloging in Publication Data
Christensen, Bonnie.
Rebus riot/ by Bonnie Christensen.—1st ed.
p.   cm.
Summary: Presents a collection of verses that
use pictures in place of some words.
ISBN 0-8037-1998-1 (trade).—ISBN 0-8037-2000-9 (lib.)
1. Children's poetry, American. 2. Rebuses—Juvenile literature.
[1. American poetry. 2. Rebuses.] I. Title.
PS3553.H697R43 1997   811'.54—dc20   96-7470   CIP   AC

The art for this book was prepared by photocopying
black-and-white scratchboard images onto paper,
which was then painted with watercolor.

The word solutions can be found at the end of the book.

PERFECT PALS

 you glad that we're a ?

For it's the  rage to share.

Whi+  around you'll always

the one who's sitting next to me.

orange   pear   currant   lime   bee

trunk   leaf

root   bark

If an elephant lost his 🌳,

he'd be in a wretched funk.

His friends and family all remind,

"You shouldn't 🍃 it far behind."

If he should want to 🌱 around,

no better tool could e'er be found.

Without a snout his bellow'd be

a woeful 🪵 and woe is he!

CRAZY DAISY

Why did 🌼 throw the clock?

She gave her 🦋 +er quite a shock.

(She threw the clock because she wanted to see time fly.)

Why did she  her brother's toe?

Well, this 🌿 we 🧅 her go.

daisy   moth

squash   thyme   shallot

🦤 dance the rumba fine.

You can spot a 🦜 anytime.

To dance the rumba all night through

is not a 🐦 thing to do.

First they're 🕊 , but then tire out,

they 🐧 pant and lie about.

Perhaps I'll spend the night at home

and leave those dancing 🐧 alone.

toucan   parrot   mynah   swift

puffin   loons

FISHY BUSINESS

KATYDID

dog   cat

sun   whale

jelly   pipe

star   squid

sail   sword

hog   sole

fish

SWEET TALK

Have you ever seen a 🐝

quite as sweet and nice as me?

Although I'm 🦡 +ly even five,

I'm still the bestest me alive.

To find me, 🍯 the fields over.

That's me singing in the 🌿.

I'm never stinging, buzzing, wild,

that's why you call me " 🐻 child."

BE MY VALENTINE

You may not 🥕 all for me

The way I care for you.

You may 🧅 your pretty nose

Whene'er I plead with you.

But if your ❤️ should 🪵 with mine,

Forever 🥬 hope,

There is no reason in the world

Why we two 🥥 .

carrot

heart

lettuce

turnip

beet

cantaloupe

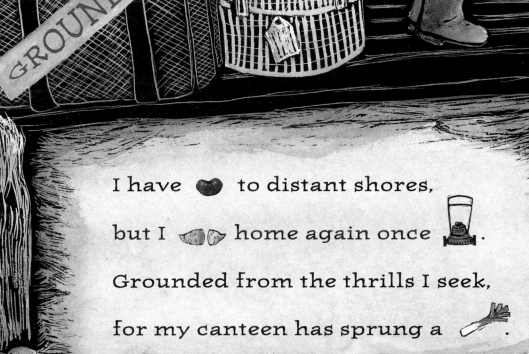

I have 🫘 to distant shores,

but I 🍠🍠 home again once 🪔.

Grounded from the thrills I seek,

for my canteen has sprung a 🥬.

bean   yam   mower   leek

MONSTER OBEDIENCE

I cannot  my monster pet.

His  tail will kill me yet.

I got him yesterday on .

They said his love would never fail.

But quickly it's becoming ,

he doesn't like this +ing game.

  him, please, for me?

Or  I will surely be.

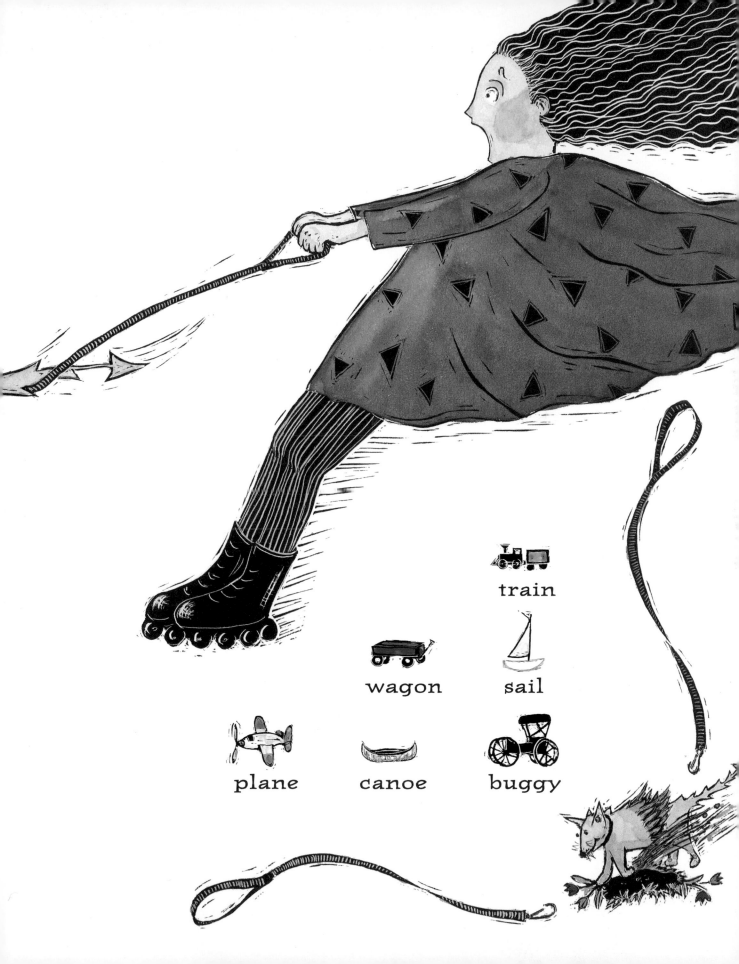

train

wagon   sail

plane   canoe   buggy

HEEBIE-JEEBIES

[owl]'ll tell you all a chilling [tail]

to make you quake, to make you [quail].

The very scary parts, my friend,

will surely stand your [heron] end.

You'll [swallow] hard and cringe with fright,

go [raven] off through darkest night.

On second thought the [tail] can wait,

I have to be back home by eight.

owl   tail

heron   swallow   raven

quail

CATalog

A cat checked out a +alog

to find a present for her dog.

The +alpa tree would be quite nice.

Who knows? It could attract some mice.

A +apult might be the thing

to show the neighbors who'd be king.

Or a +amaran, with billowed sail,

might make dear doggy wag his tail.

But a +amount, she didn't doubt,

would bring +astrophe about.

Then she'd need a +acomb.

Well...perhaps she'd leave the dog alone.

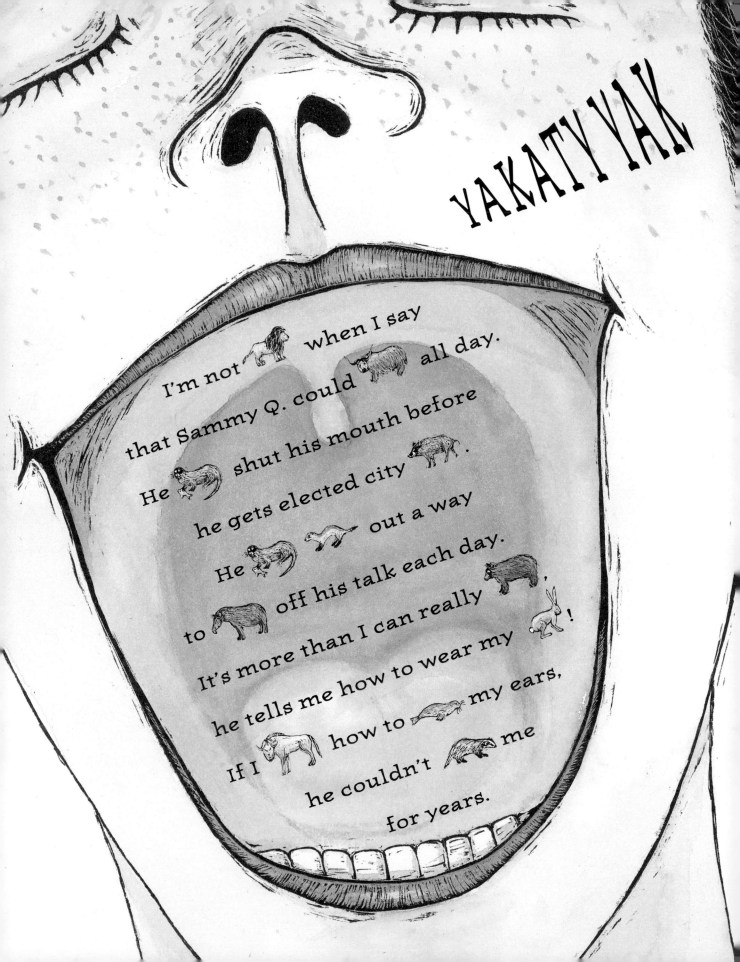

lion   yak   otter   boar   ferret

tapir   bear   hare   gnu   seal   badger

BEDBUNNIES

Though I'm the bravest kid in town,

I don't a+ [door] those nighttime sounds.

They make my courage start to [sink].

I [radio] and forget to blink.

Beneath my bed I slowly [stair].

What do you s'pose is rumbling there?

Dustbunnies big, dustbunnies small,

rowdy dustbunnies [wall] to [wall].

Should I [nail] them with my mop?

Or join them in the bunny hop?

door sink

shutter stair

wall nail

 my mom, she's so nice.

Says, " take my advice."

Says, "Sweetie pie, it's not a joke

for you to cause poor ."

Says, "Could try so very hard,

please not to make the toast so ?"

Says, "When you change the light+ , dear,

don't ask the neighbors in to cheer."

Says, "Do not shirt with ice,

I'll go   if you're not nice."

 is unknown to Mom,

'cause I'm her little sugar+ !

olive   honeydew

artichoke   yew

chard   bulb

filberts   plum

nuts   impatiens

THE TAIL END

A 's the end of the day,

A 🌲🌲🌲's the end of the plain,

The 🌙's the end of a 🐱,

The 🚃's the end of a 🚂.

It's been really swell to meet 🐑,

But if 🐑'll take a closer look,

🐑'll see that I'm saying good-bye,

'Cause 🐑've reached

the end of this... 📖.

sunset   forest   tail

   🐑 📖

dog   caboose   train   ewe   book

The Word Solutions

PERFECT PALS
Aren't you glad that we're a pair?
For it's the current rage to share.
While I'm around you'll always be
the one who's sitting next to me.

NOSING AROUND
If an elephant lost his trunk,
he'd be in a wretched funk.
His friends and family all remind,
"You shouldn't leave it far behind."
If he should want to root around,
no better tool could e'er be found.
Without a snout his bellow'd be
a woeful bark and woe is he!

CRAZY DAISY
Why did Daisy throw the clock?
She gave her mother quite a shock.
Why did she squash her brother's toe?
Well, this time we shall let her go.

BIRDIE BOOGIE
Two can dance the rumba fine.
You can spot a pair at anytime.
To dance the rumba all night through
is not a minor thing to do.
First they're swift, but then tire out,
they puff and pant and lie about.
Perhaps I'll spend the night at home
and leave those dancing loons alone.

FISHY BUSINESS
Dogfish, Catfish
Sunfish, Whale
None related to the snail.
Jellyfish, Pipefish
Starfish, Squid
Nothing like the katydid.

Sailfish, Swordfish
Hogfish, Sole
None fit in my fishy bowl.

SWEET TALK
Have you ever seen a honeybee
quite as sweet and nice as me?
Although I'm barely even five,
I'm still the bestest me alive.
To find me, comb the fields over.
That's me singing in the clover.
I'm never stinging, buzzing, wild,
that's why you call me "honey child."

BE MY VALENTINE
You may not care at all for me
The way I care for you.
You may turn up your pretty nose
Whene'er I plead with you.
But if your heart should beat with mine,
Forever let us hope,
There is no reason in the world
Why we two can't elope.

GROUNDED
I have been to distant shores,
but I am home again once more.
Grounded from the thrills I seek,
for my canteen has sprung a leak.

MONSTER OBEDIENCE
I cannot train my monster pet.
His wagging tail will kill me yet.
I got him yesterday on sale.
They said his love would never fail.
But quickly it's becoming plain,
he doesn't like this training game.
Can you train him, please, for me?
Or buggy I will surely be.

HEEBIE-JEEBIES

I'll tell you all a chilling tale
to make you quake, to make you quail.
The very scary parts, my friend,
will surely stand your hair on end.
You'll swallow hard and cringe with fright,
go raving off through darkest night.
On second thought the tale can wait,
I have to be back home by eight.

CATalog

A cat checked out a catalog
to find a present for her dog.
The catalpa tree would be quite nice.
Who knows? It could attract some mice.
A catapult might be the thing
to show the neighbors who'd be king.
Or a catamaran, with billowed sail,
might make dear doggy wag his tail.
But a catamount, she didn't doubt,
would bring catastrophe about.
Then she'd need a catacomb.
Well . . . perhaps she'd leave the dog alone.

YAKATY YAK

I'm not lying when I say
that Sammy Q. could yak all day.
He ought to shut his mouth before
he gets elected city bore.
He ought to ferret out a way
to taper off his talk each day.
It's more than I can really bear,
he tells me how to wear my hair!
If I knew how to seal my ears,
he couldn't badger me
for years.

BEDBUNNIES

Though I'm the bravest kid in town,
I don't adore those nighttime sounds.
They make my courage start to sink.
I shudder and forget to blink.
Beneath my bed I slowly stare.
What do you s'pose is rumbling there?
Dustbunnies big, dustbunnies small,
rowdy dustbunnies wall to wall.
Should I nail them with my mop?
Or join them in the bunny hop?

LITTLE PRECIOUS

I love my mom, she's so nice.
Says, "Honey, do take my advice."
Says, "Sweetie pie, it's not a joke
for you to cause poor Art to choke."
Says, "Could you try so very hard,
please not to make the toast so charred?"
Says, "When you change the lightbulb, dear,
don't ask the neighbors in to cheer."
Says, "Do not fill Bert's shirt with ice,
I'll go plumb nuts if you're not nice."
Impatience is unknown to Mom,
'cause I'm her little sugarplum!

THE TAIL END

A sunset's the end of the day,
A forest's the end of the plain,
The tail's the end of a dog,
The caboose's the end of a train.

It's been really swell to meet you,
But if you'll take a closer look,
You'll see that I'm saying good-bye,
'Cause you've reached
the end of this . . . book.